I AM....

(Positive Affirmations For Brown Girls)

By Ayesha Rodriguez

This book
is for

_____

From

_____

Library of Congress Cataloging-in-Publication Data
ISBN: 978-1-4951-9566-2 (sc)
ISBN: 978-1-4951-9565-5 (hc)

Publisher Jaye Squared Youth Empowerment Services, INC.
Website: www.ayesharodriguez.com

Illustration copyright © 2016 by Rina Risnawati

Layout Design by Susan Gulash
Gulash Graphics, Lutz, FL

This book is dedicated to my two little brown girls who inspire me to be my greatest self.
JC and JR, Mommy loves you.

TABLE OF CONTENTS

I look in the mirror and
what do I see?

I see curious, bright eyes
staring back at me.

I am special.

I woke up this morning with a smile on my face.

I have family who loves me. They can never be replaced!

I am loved.

I learn so much when
I go to school.

I can read, write and
do math too!

I think that's cool!

I am smart.

I stretch and do exercises to keep my body strong.

With water and lots of fruits and veggies, I can't go wrong!

I am healthy.

I try my best to help others who may be in need.

In life, we must plant good seeds.

I am happy.

I have really nice friends. Together
we sing, dance and play.

We have so much fun.
I could stay with them all day!

I am kind.

I have big, coiled hair and
sun-kissed brown skin.

I absolutely love the skin
that I am in!

I am beautiful.

There are no limits to
what I can achieve.

I can do anything, I just
have to believe.

I am powerful.

I am special.
I am loved.
I am smart.
I am healthy.
I am happy.
I am kind.
I am beautiful.
I am powerful.

I am a Queen.

Daily Activity:

Stand in the mirror every day and repeat all of the "I am" sentences. I want you to really believe it, just like I do! If people say things to you that are not nice, you will know in your heart that it is not true!

You are amazing and I am
so proud of you.

Discussion Questions:

1. What do you love about yourself?
2. What does love mean to you?
3. What are your favorite subjects in school?
4. What exercises do you like to do?
5. What healthy foods do you like to eat?
6. What are some good things that you have done for others?
7. What does being kind have to do with having nice friends?
8. What are you thankful for?
9. What hair styles do you like to wear?
10. We all come in different skin colors. What do you love about your brown skin?
11. What are some of your biggest dreams?
12. What makes you happy?

Are there more affirmations that you would like
to add? Write them in pencil below.

1. I am_____

2. I am_____

3. I am_____

4. I am_____

5. I am_____

6. I am_____

7. I am_____

8. I am_____

About the Author

Ayesha Rodriguez is the president of a 501c3 children's nonprofit organization, entrepreneur, author, speaker and most importantly, a mother of two. She is very passionate about education and making a positive impact in the community.

CPSIA information can be obtained
at www.ICGtesting.com
Printed in the USA
LVHW071141130720
660480LV00010BA/268